The Little Hamster Meets Soldie and Miss Strawberry In The Doll's House

Also by this author

The Little Hamster Meets Soldie and Miss Strawberry In The Doll's House

M.R. Smith

Original artwork by the author

ISBN: 9798540299589

PublishNation
www.publishnation.co.uk

The sky outside was the darkest of blue and the little stars were twinkling ever so brightly.

The little hamster, wearing his lovely warm nightshirt and his little night hat, tucked himself up in his little bed, all warm and cosy.

The teeny tiny mouse had kindly made everyone their little nightclothes from tiny scraps of materials that she had collected from the floor of the BIG house.

1

She used a little pine needle that she had picked up from the BIG garden and carefully made it into a sewing needle.

The little spider was brushing his teeth and nearly lost his tiny toothbrush because of his missing front tooth.

"Oopth!" he said, giggling a little to himself.

Then he climbed up onto his little bed, stretched his eight little hairy legs and gave a big yawn.

The little lady spider made herself comfortable in her tiny cream-coloured doll's bed with little lace frills and a tiny cream lace canopy over the top.

Tiny Ted snuggled down on a little doll's house chaise longue and covered himself in a lovely, warm blanket.

The teeny tiny mouse busied herself with tidying her tiny lace pillows, fluffing them up to make them soft and comfortable. She dusted down her pretty cream nightdress and carefully climbed into her cosy little pink bed.

As she gazed up towards the window in her little bedroom she saw all the little twinkling stars in the night sky and felt so happy in her wonderful new home with all her friends.

Suddenly, there was a squeaky little scream!

The little hamster, the teeny tiny mouse, and the two little spiders all sat straight up in their little beds, looking puzzled, wondering what the squeaky little scream was.

It seemed to be coming from one of the chimneys on the roof of the doll's house. So, the little hamster and the teeny tiny mouse decided to go downstairs to find out what was going on.

The two little spiders stayed in the little bedroom and listened by the fireplace, just in case the squeaky little scream returned.

The little hamster and the teeny tiny mouse, wearing their little, warm nightclothes, carefully walked outside the doll's house. The squeaky little scream began to get louder.

They both stood back and looked up at the doll's house and saw two long legs sticking out of one of the chimneys!

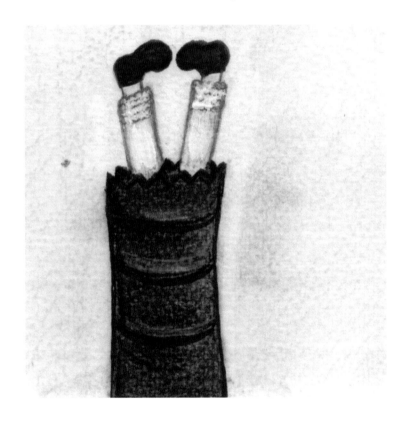

"Oh crumbs!" exclaimed the little hamster worriedly.

The teeny tiny mouse put her little lace handkerchief over her tiny eyes in shock.

The two little friends were puzzled as to what to do, but they knew that the long legs stuck up in the air needed some help!

Then, all the lights in the doll's house came on and out walked Tiny Ted, and beside him walked a small, very fine soldier doll.

Tiny Ted introduced the very fine soldier doll as Soldie, as that was what he was called by the children in the BIG house.

The little hamster and the teeny tiny mouse were very relieved to see help arrive. But how was he going to get the long legs out of the chimney?

"What are we going to do?" said the little hamster, looking very puzzled indeed.

"Oh goodness," remarked the teeny tiny mouse, still holding her little lace handkerchief up to her little eyes.

Meanwhile, the two little spiders scurried up to the attic room, as that was the closest room to the roof of the doll's house and its chimneys.

The little spider nearly lost his tiny nightcap as he was running so fast, his eight little legs hardly catching up with each other!

The little lady spider ran behind him, holding her little nightdress up slightly, so as not to tread on the pretty lace.

As they entered the attic room in the doll's house, the squeaky scream became louder. It was definitely coming from the fireplace!

The little spider, taking off his tiny nightcap, climbed up inside the chimney.

"Oh, please be careful!" said the little lady spider in a very worried and delicate voice.

Very soon, the little spider scurried back down as fast as his little legs could carry him.

Puffing and panting, he turned to the little lady spider and fearfully said, "Thewe's a very stwange face at the top of the chimney and I am not sure about it!"

In the meantime, the little friends and Soldie went up to the attic room.

The little hamster could see the little spider was still puffing and panting.

Soldie decided they should go up inside the chimney and pull whatever it was out that way.

"But how will we do that?" exclaimed the little hamster worriedly.

"I will do it!" said the little spider as he gazed towards the little lady spider, giving her a big grin with his missing front tooth. The little lady spider smiled sweetly at him, fluttering her little soft eyelashes.

Soldie organised everyone to stand guard at the bottom of the fireplace in the attic room, whilst the little spider climbed up inside the chimney. He began trembling as he got closer to the very strange face.

Just then, the lady spider climbed up beside him. She almost jumped as she, too, saw the very strange face!

The strange face, all dusty black with soot, gave a big smile, and as she did so, her white teeth dazzled the little spiders!

The little spiders began to spin their silky webs around the dangling arms of the thing with the very strange face, and as they did so, they spun more webs to lower themselves slowly down the chimney into the fireplace.

All the little friends looked on in amazement. Then the little hamster ran forward to move the tiny fire in the fireplace out of the way in order to make room for the little spiders.

Soldie looked up towards the very strange face with the white teeth. He appeared a little concerned.

He held out his arms and everyone heard a loud thump as the thing with the very strange face and the white teeth landed!

A very sad and pitiful-looking doll appeared wearing a red and white checkered dress with a little white apron and a little red and white checkered hat, all now dusty black with soot.

She gave a little sneeze as she looked at everyone staring at her.

Soldie smiled and politely introduced her as Miss Strawberry.

"What were you doing in the chimney?" asked the little hamster politely.

Miss Strawberry, trying not to cry, told the little friends that she was looking for her present as she believed Father Christmas may have accidentally got it stuck down the chimney.

Oh dear! All the little friends looked sad.

The teeny tiny mouse ran over to Miss Strawberry and began dusting her sooty clothes with her little fluffy duster.

"You are so kind," said Miss Strawberry, gratefully, now feeling a bit silly, not to mention a little ashamed of herself.

Miss Strawberry thanked the little spiders ever so much for rescuing her. A little tear rolled down her black, sooty cheek.

Soldie gently took hold of her hand and led her out of the attic.

The little hamster put the little fire back in its place, whilst the teeny tiny mouse kindly swept up all the soot.

Everyone returned to their beds, but it wasn't long before the little spider woke everyone up again with his loud snoring!

"It's been a very long night and I am sure the little spider is ever so tired," remarked the little hamster, smiling to everyone now sitting up in their little beds.

Meanwhile, the teenie-weenie angel flew upstairs to see Miss Strawberry, who was sitting by a little bed in another room. She was so very sad.

"I'm just an old rag doll," said Miss Strawberry with little tears in her eyes. "Everyone forgets about rag dolls."

The teenie-weenie angel gently waved her magic wand and all the dusty soot flew away off of Miss Strawberry.

Standing at the little bedroom door was Soldie, and he was smiling sweetly at Miss Strawberry.

The teenie-weenie angel looked at Soldie, then turned and spoke gently to Miss Strawberry.

"You see," said the teenie-weenie angel in her sweet teenie-weenie voice, "it's not all about presents, but about love. You have someone here who loves you, and all your little newfound friends love you, too."

The teenie-weenie angel continued, "Love is the best gift of all."

Soldie walked slowly over to Miss Strawberry and gently took hold of her hand.

The two dolls then carefully sat down on an old doll's house settee, falling peacefully asleep with their little heads softly resting against each other.

Miss Strawberry and Soldie, now fast asleep, didn't realise that all their little friends were standing at the little bedroom door watching them with tears in their little eyes.

The teeny tiny mouse quietly scurried over, grabbed a little soft blanket, and gently covered them both to keep them snug and warm.

Everyone else then returned to their beds and they all fell sound asleep.

It must have been a few hours later that Miss Strawberry slowly woke up. By her little foot she saw a small box, beautifully wrapped with a pretty red bow and ribbons.

Attached to the small box was a little hand-written note which read:

Dear Miss Strawberry,

As we were flying away, Rudolph complained that something was rattling in my sack, so we decided to land in a field not too far away. I really hope that you can forgive me. I am very, very, very old and sometimes very forgetful these days.

But that is no excuse for bad manners. Rudolph is smiling at me as I am writing this, and once again, I am really sorry.

You are never, ever forgotten.

Lots of Love,
Father Christmas

Miss Strawberry was so excited! But, she also remembered what the teenie-weenie angel had told her, and very quietly opened her little present.

Father Christmas had kindly given her a beautiful shawl with little roses upon it. She carefully wrapped it around her little shoulders and snuggled next to her Soldie, once more.

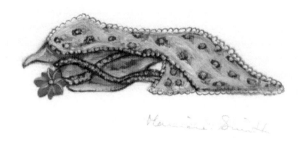

"You see," whispered the teenie-weenie angel, "it has never been forgotten, that very cold night that you left the doll's house in your beautiful shawl with the little roses upon it, and you slipped it through the little hamster's cage, softly covering him with it, as he was shivering so much from the cold."

The teenie-weenie angel flew upstairs to see all the little creatures tucked up safely in their beds.

As she did so, she waved her magic wand over the little spider as he slept, for she knew of the kindness he showed in helping others.

In the morning when he wakes up, he will know that he has been given a lovely new front tooth, and upon his little pillow, a teenie-weenie note thanking him.

As the morning sun was slowly rising, lighting up the snow like tiny crystals which sparkled upon the gardens and on the trees and bushes of the BIG house, the sound of sweet singing from the little birds could be heard in the large tree outside the BIG window.

Yet, all was quiet in the doll's house as everyone was still fast asleep.

All except the little hamster, who sat up in his cosy little bed, smiling happily, realising how lucky and thankful he was to have all his wonderful friends around him.

So, whenever there is love and kindness to animals, and to each other, there is always a teenie-weenie angel watching over you, smiling sweetly.

And who knows what magical gifts she will bring to you!

Printed in Great Britain
by Amazon